A DASH OF PEPPER

K.F. JONES

CHAPTER 1

"Amber, have you finished eating?" Mistress Susanna asked.

"Yes, thank you, Mistress," Amber replied.

"Then it's time for you to go for your night in the stables, don't you think?"

"As you wish, Mistress," Amber said, meekly, as Sugar and Candy began clearing the big kitchen table.

"Oh, are you going to go and have some fun with the ponies?" Candy asked.

"Why don't you explain, Amber?" Susanna said darkly.

Amber nodded and began to relate the story, "I was naughty when I raced Mistress around the lake yesterday. I'm to go to the stables and give myself to Pepper and Ginger for the night."

Pudding chimed in, "Think yourself lucky, it doesn't sound like the worst of punishments."

"I know plenty of women who'd love to belong to those two for a night," Roxy agreed.

Amber blushed. "Mistress has ordered that they can punish me or use me for their pleasure as they see fit."

"I'm pretty sure they'll just want to be pleasured," Sugar pointed out.

Amber shook her head, "No, Pepper was already punished for letting me bribe her."

"Yes, she'll definitely want her pound of flesh. Pepper has a vindictive streak. It sounds like you have a tough night ahead of you. How wonderful," Pudding said. She sighed dreamily, clearly imagining what awaited Amber.

"Mistress, could I go too? It sounds like it would be entertaining to watch," Candy asked.

Susanna frowned, "It's not about Amber getting used for your amusement."

"I'd like to go too, Mistress. I'd love to see Amber get her comeuppance for being so naughty," Sugar said.

"You both want to go?" Susanna grumbled. "I'm giving Ginger and Pepper free rein to punish and use Amber for the whole night if they wish. It may be a long night."

Candy shrugged, "Maybe we could just go for a while and then leave them to it?" Sugar nodded in agreement.

"No, if you go, you'll be under the same rules as Amber. You'll belong to Ginger and Pepper to do with as they wish all night," Susanna said with a wickedly dark grin. Amber could sense the challenge in her decree.

Candy chewed her lip and Sugar just looked excited replying, "Yes, Mistress. Please can I go?"

Susanna sighed and threw her napkin to the table in a huff, "I should have known you two sluts wouldn't back down from that. Fine, you can both go, but you make sure the girls understand that Amber is the one with a debt to pay, and I expect them to extract their due. You can be a reward on top."

"Thank you, Mistress," Sugar and Candy chorused.

"Enough, sluts. Get out of my sight," Susanna said, turning toward Roxy and Pudding.

As Amber left the kitchen, she turned at the doorway, to see Roxy crawling on the floor toward Mistress and Pudding lowering herself over her knee.

Clearly Mistress Susanna was going to have her own fun this evening.

❧

They found Ginger and Pepper upstairs at the stables, resting in their small flat after their evening meal.

"Hello, you lot, what's up?" Ginger, the elegant redhead asked. Amber was surprised to see the pony girls wearing normal clothes. They were both relaxing in shorts and t-shirts, on a big sofa in front of the TV. Amber had only seen them dressed in their pony fetish gear before, which concealed far less of their sexy bodies, and they were also in character as ponies as well.

It was jarring to find them in a setting like any other twenty-something young woman enduring an evening at home, sitting down and watching whatever was on TV.

"Mistress has a gift for you," Candy leered.

Pepper and Ginger both perked up at this news, and Pepper picked up the remote to switch off the TV.

"Oh yes?" Ginger replied. "What kind of gift?"

"I present to you, Amber Hannam, personal assistant to Susanna Hamilton. Mistress wanted you both to know that as Amber was naughty yesterday, this evening, she belongs to you. You may punish her, and use her for your pleasure all night," Candy said.

Ginger turned to Pepper with a broad grin, "Nice. Revenge!"

Pepper giggled.

"Mistress wanted it to be clear that Amber has a debt to pay, and that she expects you to extract your full due for her naughtiness during the race and the punishment that Pepper received as a result," Sugar added.

Like a game show host trying to hype up a seemingly mediocre prize, Candy continued, "But wait, there's more! You also win a night with Mistress Susanna's favourite maids, Sugar and Candy. You'll get one whole night with all three girls, to do with as you wish. Spank them, ride their tongues or force orgasm after orgasm from their hot, wet pussies, the choice is yours!"

Amber laughed out loud and the other girls joined in. It was a nice try, planting the suggestions in the ponies minds like that but she wondered if it would backfire. Perhaps it would lead Ginger and Pepper to everything but those options for Sugar and Candy.

"What do you think, Ginger?"

"I think we'd better do as Mistress ordered, Pepper," Ginger said.

Pepper waved her hand at the three girls who had presented themselves for punishment.

"Strip!"

CHAPTER 2

"First, let's put Sugar and Candy out of the way," Pepper said.

"What did you have in mind?" Ginger asked, gesturing at the playroom area in the stables. It was filled with all sorts of possibilities.

A few minutes later, Sugar and Candy were naked, lying bottom to bottom on a long padded bench, their heads resting on the last few inches of the furniture. Pepper had put Amber on her knees where the maid's hips faced each other.

"Get this into them both," Pepper said, handing Amber a large, doubled headed dildo that was thick and felt heavy in her hand.

Amber obediently complied, licking her lips and sizing up which maid to start with. She had never done this before and the thing wasn't as flexible as she would have guessed. It didn't flop as she held it by one end but remained ramrod straight.

Settling on Sugar first, Amber put the fingers of one hand on the maid's labia and parted them, revealing her target.

"She's not wet enough, use your tongue," Pepper ordered,

standing above Amber and lashing her buttocks with a riding crop for emphasis. Amber winced but put her tongue obediently to work, lapping fast to get Sugar suitably excited.

"That's hot," Candy said before Ginger sat on her face and muffled her voice.

Amber had received a full dozen strokes of the riding crop split evenly across her buttocks before she put the dildo at Sugar's pussy and found it easily slid home. Candy was already wet from watching Amber lick her fellow maid and in turn, the ecstasy of licking Ginger.

Positioning her hips was tricky but Amber was eventually able to get the tip of the dildo in, and then move the maids together until their buttocks touched. Their thighs were upright and pressed against their counterparts, but both at eleven o'clock from their view, so they were offset. Pepper used a thick leather strap and buckle to secure Sugar's leg to Candy's and the girls were lift spreadeagled, a big silicone cock joining them, with their legs up in the air. Their calves weren't restricted so they fell at ninety degrees.

"Now, turn it on," Pepper said.

Amber looked at her in confusion and Pepper sighed melodramatically, pointing at the silicone rod. Amber inspected it more closely and realised that a black disc in the middle section could be rotated. Twisting it, the whole thing began to vibrate gently. Sugar and Candy immediately began to squirm.

"More, turn it up to the max," Pepper said.

Ginger giggled, "Oh, that's just cruel."

"It's only what Mistress would want, anyway, we have to concentrate on Amber," Pepper said, diverting any blame from her. She was innocent. This was all at the behest of their Mistress, after all.

The control turned, and the vibration became more intense. Amber kept going until it wouldn't turn any more and Sugar was moaning loudly. Candy's response was still muffled by Ginger's pussy, but she seemed to be enjoying it.

"Gag these bitches," Pepper said in an effort to sound imperious as she handed Amber two big red ball gags.

Starting with Sugar, Amber popped the ball into the maid's mouth and buckled the strap firmly behind her head. Ginger looked a little cross at having to dismount Candy, but the second maid was soon moaning around the rubber sphere which filled her mouth.

"There, that should keep them occupied," Pepper said, clapping her hands with satisfaction.

Both ponies turned menacing looks on Amber.

"What do you want to do with her?" Ginger asked.

"I think she should try a nice standing pose for her punishment, don't you?"

"It's your party, Pepper. You're the one who got punished for this slut. Whatever you say is good with me," Ginger said.

The two ponies soon had Amber standing, her wrists cuffed close together in heavily padded, thick leather cuffs. The chain linking the cuffs was clipped into a carabiner, and then Candy pulled on a rope that dangled from a pulley attached to the ceiling. Amber's hands were lifted above her.

Pepper attached what she called a spreader bar to Amber's ankles. It was just a long black rod, with ankle cuffs at either end. It forced Amber's feet a little over shoulder-width apart. Once that was done, Candy adjusted the rope holding her wrists.

Amber ended up just having to stand as upright as possible, or she'd have to get up on tiptoe if she didn't want to find herself dangling from the ceiling.

"What do you want to use?" Ginger asked, gesturing at the toys.

Pepper began making a show of picking up and inspecting various implements that Amber had used to punish her under Susanna's instruction just the day before. Each one she found fault with and discarded. Ginger held her head by the hair at the back and her chin, using both hands to make sure Amber had to watch the pony select her punishment.

"How about this, Ginger?"

"Looks good to me. I haven't seen it used in a while," Ginger replied.

"No. Most people find it a bit scary, Amber. But I'm sure it'll be lovely to see Ginger use this carpet beater on you," Pepper mused, handing the large rattan cleaning implement to the other pony and chuckling to herself.

In the background, Sugar and Candy seemed insensible as their bodies were wracked with orgasms.

"What are you going to do while I use this, Pepper?" Ginger asked curiously, stroking the carpet beater across Amber's buttocks so she couldn't forget what was coming.

Pepper turned around from where she'd been inspecting the toys on offer and stepped forward, holding up a wicked looking pair of nipples clamps with a thin chain linking them.

"I think these would look gorgeous on Amber's perky nipples, don't you?"

"Yes, I have to agree," Ginger giggled.

Amber shook her head, "No, please, Pepper, don't!"

The ponygirl had no mercy for her though, and the clamps were soon closing on her treacherously stiff nipples. Amber squealed at the pain. Pepper hooked one finger over the chain and pulled it towards herself with until it tugged gently on Amber's nipples. Amber whimpered at the change in sensation.

"You can thrash her now, Ginger," Pepper said, blowing a kiss to Amber. "If you wriggle too much, your nipples will let you know about it, Amber."

The carpet beater made a fearsome whooshing sound as it

powered through the air, and alighted on Amber's curvaceous bottom with a clatter of the rattan weave.

Amber cried out in pain and Pepper laughed, "Count them out, slut. Or Ginger will start again."

Ginger thrashed her again, and Amber howled, "Two!"

"No, you start from one, Amber, and say 'Thank you, Ginger,' after each one," Pepper insisted, tugging on the chain to reinforce her demand.

When the carpet beater struck her a third time, Amber whimpered and spat out, "One! Thank you, Ginger."

"Good, now you have it. Keep going," Pepper said.

As Ginger beat her bottom with the long-handled implement, Amber counted out the full dozen strokes. Pepper leaned in and stoppered the sound of her pain with a deep kiss. Hungrily, the pony's tongue writhed against hers as her hand caressed Amber's neck.

"What's next, Mistress?" Ginger asked.

Pepper chuckled at the unearned title, "I'm not sure."

"Would you like her to eat your pussy?" Ginger suggested.

Pepper pretended to consider that for a few minutes. "I suppose, if I must for her punishment to be carried out," Pepper said. "How do you want me?"

"Let's move that bench over and let her hands down a bit," Ginger suggested.

Soon, Pepper was lying on a bench, her pussy presented toward Amber. The rope keeping her upright was slowly lowered until Amber could drop to her knees. Quickly, she shuffled forward and began to lick at Pepper's glistening lips with abandon, eager to avoid additional punishment.

Ginger returned the carpet beater to the rack, which gave Amber a small glimmer of hope until she selected a long, thin cane which she immediately applied to Amber's bottom with dramatic, swishing strokes.

Pepper had to put her hand behind Amber's head to keep her firmly clamped in place, as each stroke caused her to buck up in discomfort. "Keep licking, slut," Pepper ordered.

A dozen strokes later and Pepper hadn't come, but Amber felt unbelievably wet. She was convinced she could feel dribbles of her arousal running down her thighs.

In any case, when Ginger stood next to Pepper so Amber could see her buckling up a leather harness and selecting a big dildo, Amber had an idea of what to expect.

The application of a flogger to her back wasn't it. Amber spluttered and whined as she tried to eat Pepper's pussy properly, as Ginger's flogger began reddening her back. It was an entirely different kind of pain for her to get used to, and Ginger wasn't sparing her.

Pepper was soon coming, her hips bucking and grinding against Amber's face as she shouted encouraging but obscene suggestions to Amber.

When the pony started to subside, and her grip loosened, Amber was able to gulp in some big lungfuls of air. Then she found herself gasping again for another reason. Ginger had lined up a dildo at her entrance and began to push it slowly past the barrier of her wet folds.

Ginger was fucking her hard with the big strap-on, as Pepper's panting subsided and she smiled down at Amber. "Again, slut," Pepper ordered, forcing Amber's head down with both hands as if Amber really needed to be forced to give her pleasure. Amber would have done it, just for the asking, but she knew the girls were getting off on tormenting her, perhaps not as much as Pudding or Mistress Susanna would, but they were really enjoying themselves.

Amber felt her own orgasm arise and when she'd screamed her passion into Pepper's pussy, the young maid laughed and ordered her to bring her to an orgasm as good as that one.

Her tongue was put back to work and Amber barely noticed the addition of Ginger's lubricated finger to her puckered hole at first, but the second certainly got her attention.

Amber lifted her head and moaned, "Fuck! That's so dirty."

"Quiet, slut," Pepper ordered as Ginger worked a third finger into Amber's arsehole. Amber could do nothing but lick and make muffled noises of approval into Pepper's pussy.

"She loves it, doesn't she?" Ginger stated.

"She certainly does. Think she can take the foxtail?"

"Probably, she's gaping for me," Ginger said. "It might be a bit uncomfortable though, do you think we should?"

It took Pepper a moment to respond clearly as another orgasm rocked her body, but when she eventually could, she replied, "Yes, hang on."

Pepper got up and pulled something from a toy drawer, presenting it to Amber so she could see it clearly.

"See how big this is, Amber? This is going into your tight bumhole. Would you like that?"

"No, please, Pepper," Amber begged. The plug seemed enormous to her, looming in front of her eyes, bigger than anything she'd taken so far. Pepper smirked at her.

"You'll take it, and you'll like it, Amber. I bet you'll hate it at first, but you'll soon be begging for more," Pepper boasted. "You always have your safe word if you need it." Pepper made her last point rather smugly, seemingly confident that Amber would do no such thing.

When Ginger began to probe her with the big plug, she came close to shouting out her safe word, several times in fact. It was uncomfortable being stretched so much and the maid was still slowly fucking her with the strap-on, which was also not a small example of its kind.

Amber found it hard to concentrate on her duty of licking Pepper, as the butt plug slowly pushed at her tight ring of muscle, then eased off a bit before Ginger pressed it firmly into her anus again. Amber lost track of time as the butt plug was slowly worked deeper and deeper into her as she brought Pepper to multiple orgasms.

All the while, the thick silicone cock was pumping back and forth in her pussy and Amber reached her own climax at least twice.

Ginger cried out excitedly when the plug finally slid forward, past the widest section and Amber felt her ring close around the narrow portion. "It's in Pepper! The slut took it all," Ginger said.

"Good girl, Amber. Well done," Pepper congratulated her. "How are you two doing?" she called over to Sugar and Candy who were both flushed and perspiring. "Hey, has the battery run out on that thing?" Ginger asked.

Sugar nodded weakly, her eyes unfocused and unable to speak intelligibly around the big ball gag.

"We'll have to sort that out in a while," Pepper said. "First, I think you should enjoy Amber's tongue too, Ginger."

Ginger pulled back and had the strap-on harness off, quick as a flash. Pepper stood up to make way, and Amber soon found herself with a new pussy to worship.

"The night is young ladies," Pepper said. "Anyone feeling tired?"

"Not me," Ginger purred as Amber lapped at her hungrily. "Amber's so eager to please. No wonder Mistress has been neglecting us."

"Yes, we should spank her for that," Pepper said.

"Yes, she hasn't been spanked yet, has she?" Ginger agreed. Amber's possible complaint couldn't be heard past the thighs of the pony who was tightly clamped around her head, greedily demanding her own orgasms.

"No. But first, give me the strap-on, Ginger. I want to fuck her too," Pepper said.

"Here you go. Are you going to take her hard and fast, or slow and gentle?"

"Slow. We have all night, after all. But not gently," Pepper replied. "You'd like that, wouldn't you, Amber?"

Ginger let Amber lift her head to answer briefly.

"Yes, Pepper."

CHAPTER 3

"That's right, bend her over the arch," Pepper said.

Amber struggled, but she was no match for Sugar, Candy and Ginger all at once. They soon had her stretched back over an item that looked a bit like one of the various padded spanking benches in the room, with one difference. It followed a curved, rather than flat line, which was so curved that it almost described a full semi-circle.

Since Amber was now bent back over it and was being strapped down, she was grateful for the small mercy that it more of half a squashed circle, than an actual one. Still, her head was below her shoulders, which were below the midpoint, which was somewhere between her bust and her belly button.

A collar was fastened around her neck, and a short chain attached to it, then clipped to the bench, leaving her just a few inches of play to move her head side to side or up and down.

A strap was passed over her waist and buckled down tight. Her bottom was on one large area of padding, and then her thighs and legs were each on their own, long board, which the girls soon cuffed them too. Pepper stepped forward and removed a couple of locking pins, "Spread your legs wide, slut."

Amber swallowed but a quick slap on her belly, which stung like anything, produced the desired response and she spread her legs as wide as she could. Pepper rammed the locking pins home again, keeping the boards which supported her legs, held in a Y shape at the widest point that Amber could manage.

The curve of the bench was just shallow enough to not be painful, but Amber did feel quite vulnerable and extremely exposed. The butt plug with the foxtail attached to it was still buried in her arse, and her puffy lips, swollen by hours of arousal, were wet with anticipation as the girls stood around her, admiring her body.

"Look how used she looks," Candy said.

"Mmm. It's so sexy seeing her like this," Sugar agreed.

"I'm glad you approve, Candy. Get on your knees and tease her with your tongue. I want her begging for release, but don't let her come, or I'll give you such a spanking," Pepper warned.

"Yes, Miss," Candy said, seemingly entirely happy with the instruction.

"Ginger, any requests?" Pepper asked.

"I'd like to play with Sugar for a bit if you have no objection. You can have Amber all to yourself."

"That's fine with me," Pepper said.

Ginger rounded on Sugar in a flash and hurried her over to a machine attached to a bench, on which she soon had the maid strapped down to on her belly. Some adjustments were made, and Ginger sat down on a chair in front of Sugar, positioning herself within reach of the maid's willing tongue. Then she thumbed the remote she'd picked up and the machine began to turn an axle to which two wheels were attached, that rested just under a foot from Sugar's buttocks.

Amber could see what was happening by turning her head. The wheels each had a couple of leather strap attached to it, and once they began to spin around, they slapped down across Sugar's buttocks with a bottom wobbling crack of noise.

Sugar cried out at the sudden shock of it,

"What the hell is that?" Amber found herself saying.

"The machine? It doesn't have an official name yet. We just call it The Slapper," Pepper replied.

"Where did it come from?" Amber asked.

"Ginger is an engineering student. This is a project she's been doing since she went on sabbatical so she can serve Mistress Susanna," Pepper explained, crouching beside Amber and reaching out to torment her nipples with pinches and tugs. It was hard enough talking past the pleasure that Candy's wickedly skilful tongue was bringing to her, but the pain Pepper inflicted had her gasping and her eyes filling with water.

"She took a break from university to serve Mistress Susanna?"

"I certainly did," Ginger called out, even as Sugar howled into her pussy.

Pepper straddled Amber's head, "Yes. The Mistress is extremely persuasive. I used to be an English student, but I gave it up entirely to serve Mistress. I can do a degree later in life, but I may only have a few years to enjoy this lifestyle before I'm no longer attractive enough."

"Don't be silly, Pepper. Mistress Susanna isn't going to abandon you when you hit thirty, you know," Ginger snorted, before crying out as Sugar brought her to orgasm.

Pepper nodded as she simultaneously pinched and twisted both of Amber's nipples, causing her to whimper in pain.

"Maybe. Either way, a few years of pure fun now doesn't stop me from doing other things later. Now, Amber, are you quite finished with questions for now?"

"Yes, Pepper," Amber said. It was a lie, but she could see how wet Pepper was, and the sound of Sugar crying tears of exhilaration as she was spanked by the machine and licked Ginger's pussy was making her even hornier. That is, if it was possible to be hornier than having Candy teasing her clit with her tongue and lips. Amber wondered how many times Susanna had made the girls torment each other, denying them the release of orgasm. They were certainly experts at getting her close to the edge, then pulling back. Was there an official training course or something?

Without another word, Pepper's wet lips descended on Amber's mouth and there was no more conversation to be had. Amber began to lick the length of Pepper's delicious sex and suck the fleshy labia between her lips, teasing and tempting her before she moved on.

Pepper's mouth descended to kiss Amber's stomach as she found the maid's clit and sucked on it hard.

The cries of ecstasy reverberated around the room, set to the beat of the leather straps flailing against Sugar's hot pink bottom.

"Yes, just like that, Amber. Oh, Ginger, she's getting better all the time," Pepper said as she threw her head back and moaned when Amber's attentions hit exactly the right spot.

"Yes, she is good, isn't she? I think Sugar and Candy have been helping train her up," Ginger suggested.

"Definitely. I'm coming already," Pepper agreed.

Amber took that as a cue and redoubled her efforts, causing Pepper to yelp in shock as she started to shudder her way into a huge climax. As Pepper tried to rise and finish her orgasm, Amber wrapped her arms around her thighs and clamped her to her face. Her tongue continued to lap fiercely at Pepper's pussy throughout her orgasm, and though the pony struggled Amber did not relent.

"Let go of me!" Pepper protested. "I'm too sensitive."

But Amber didn't want to let go, she wanted to make Pepper come. After all, the pony had a safeword too.

By the time she did finally relent, Pepper was close to sobbing from the delightful torment that Amber had wreaked on her with a row of shattering orgasms. Her knees were weak and she almost stumbled.

Amber dropped her head to the padding of the bench and laughed triumphantly.

Ginger switched off the machine that had been punishing Sugar and began to unstrap the maid.

Pepper dropped to her knees and then to all fours, gasping for a few minutes as she recovered. Finally, she stopped up, towering over the prone Amber.

"Candy, sit back. She's not to come at all!" Pepper snapped crossly.

Pepper came around and stood over Amber's head, so she could see that she was strapping on a dildo again. This one was bigger, and misshapen, with strange whorls and protrusions along its length.

Candy sat beside Amber, watching with interest, then Ginger and Sugar joined her.

Once it was firmly in place, Pepper presented it to Amber's lips. "Suck it," she ordered.

Amber did her best, but she could barely squeeze the thing between her lips and Pepper wasn't gentle about it. Desperately she flexed her jaws as best she could and tried to open herself to the intrusion, but she still coughed and spluttered. Pepper withdrew before she choked.

"Too big for you, slut?"

Amber spluttered, "Yes."

Pepper grinned down at her and walked around to the other end, then pressed the tip of the big cock to Ambers other lips. "Let's try this way then. I'm sure you can open for my little toy, can't you, Amber?"

Amber was so wet by then that the tip pushed inside her with relative ease, though she grunted and whimpered as it filled her completely. Pepper pushed her hips forward and buried it completely in just a few progressive thrusts.

"That's it, good girl," Pepper purred, stroking Amber's thighs. "Comfortable?"

Amber groaned, "No, Pepper."

"Great! Mistress Susanna will be pleased to hear that," Pepper said with evident glee as she began to push back and forth, taking Amber in long, even strokes.

"Pleased?" Amber whimpered as the thick length of silicone plunged into her, again and again.

Pepper grunted with the effort, "Yes. This is one of her favourite types of toys. She loves to take me and Ginger with it. When I tell her I got to break you in with it, she'll be jealous. Jealous, but happy."

"She certainly will," Ginger agreed.

"Help me out, ladies," Pepper ordered.

Sugar and Candy came forward eagerly, their hot mouths clamping down on Amber's aching nipples. Ginger bent over her to kiss her lips. Amber felt herself floating away with the overwhelming sensation of it all.

Pepper took hold of Amber's hips and began to ride her faster and it wasn't long before Amber was coming, crying out in ecstasy as Ginger lifted her head. The ride didn't stop until she'd reached her third orgasm though, as Pepper was clearly keen on getting her revenge.

The girls had to help Amber to the corner sofa once she'd been unstrapped because she couldn't stand on her own.

"Thank you, Pepper. That was lovely," Amber said.

"You're welcome, Sexy," Pepper said. "Thank you for taking it all so well. I hope everyone feels able to report to Mistress that Amber was sufficiently punished, yes?"

The girls all agreed that Amber had been well punished indeed.

Amber curled up on the sofa, her head in Pepper's lap. Pepper stroked her hair gently.

"I didn't think it was that bad a punishment," Amber said.

"No? You could have taken more?" Pepper asked, amused.

"Maybe just a dash more, Pepper," Amber replied. Then she yelped as Pepper hauled her over her lap. "Hey!"

"You're mine for the whole night, Amber," Pepper reminded her.

"But, you said I've been punished properly," Amber protested. Peppers hand connected with her rump firmly, and Amber squealed.

"The night's not over yet, Amber. This bottom doesn't look well seasoned to me," Pepper said. "I think you need at least a bit more play, a sprinkle of orgasms here, a round of spanking there, perhaps?"

"Maybe just a dash more, Pepper."

AUTHOR'S NOTE

Thank you for reading A Dash of Pepper, Book One of Amber's Culinary Adventures.

If you enjoyed the book and can spare the time to leave a review on Amazon or Goodreads, I would greatly appreciate it.

Positive and constructive feedback and comments, even a simple star rating, are a great way to let me know that you want to read more about these characters.

This series is about Amber, and the other women in service to Susanna Hamilton, a wealthy lesbian with a hedonistic lifestyle.

Miss Hamilton has a taste for games of domination and submission, and employs Amber to be her new Personal Assistant.

Amber has never gone beyond an active fantasy life, and actually played with another woman. Susanna offers the twin temptations of a much needed job and pleasures Amber has never tasted.

News and Updates

One of my goals for 2020 is to be far more productive in every area of my writing. I made a rod for my own back in 2019 (not the kinky kind, sadly) by trying to do too many projects at once.

This year, I want to finish off old projects, and focus on one or two at a time, rather than six or seven.

You can read a longer and more informative version of these author notes at the end of Shared by Her Lesbian Boss (Book 5).

If you want to chime in, support me, or get updates, I'm pretty active on Twitter at the moment.

Thanks, K.F. Jones

Amber and Susanna

The main series, Submissive Lesbian Personal Assistant, which details how Amber meets Susanna and becomes her lesbian submissive, is now complete as of April 2020.

The entire six book series of Submissive Lesbian Personal Assistant, is now available in one bundle at the bargain price of $0.99.

Her Lesbian Boss: The Complete Box Set

It will conclude the first story arc for Amber and Susanna. If the series and its companion series go well, I'll be able to write a second story arc later in the year.

Amber's Culinary Adventures

A Dash of Peppers is the first book in Amber's Culinary

Adventures, which I announced in the notes for Shared by Her Lesbian Boss.

Don't worry, none of them will actually be about cooking.

Here are some of the working titles - see if they whet your appetite:

- A Dash of Pepper - Book 1
- A Sprinkling of Sugar
- A Taste of Pudding
- A Filling of Ginger

The Culinary Adventures are going to be erotic shorts about an encounter Amber has with one or more of her friends.

As with this book, I'll release them as individual works, £0.99/$0.99 as well as making them available in Kindle Unlimited.

Once I have enough, I'll release an omnibus volume which will making buying them outright even cheaper.

Here's a summary:

- A series of erotic stories about Amber
- Short, one or two scenes, 5K words
- $0.99/£0.99 individually
- Omnibus to follow
- Seven outlined so far!

These shorts will help me provide extra content, expand the world and story but not overwhelm me in the same way multiple larger projects/series did last year.

Hellcats Academy - Izzy & Kaos

Carlotta Black and I are working on a completely revamped version of the Hellcat Academy series and will relaunch it in due course. Watch this space.

Let Me Know What You Think

For those of you who have Kindle Unlimited, you can borrow all my books and, if you want to read them again at some point, you'll be able to borrow the omnibus editions so they don't use up lots of slots in your Kindle library.

Don't forget to let me know if you want me to prioritise writing more of the Lesbian Boss series, over say, finishing the Sexy Student Lessons series or adding another quartet to my Consort of the Werewolf King series.

I'm quite active on Twitter at the moment though it's not safe for work, so be warned.

It's a pretty good place to reach me as I write this (Feb 2020) if you want to support me, talk about the books, or let me know which of my series I should concentrate on.

Thanks for your support, and for buying the book or borrowing it through Kindle Unlimited.

Yours steamily,

K.F. Jones

I have several series in the works, so I have something for everyone. You can read about first time gay werewolves, steampunk heroines, students exploring their sexuality, lesbian espionage agents or young women discovering they have a taste for submitting to older lesbians.

Consort of the Werewolf King

Will has just broken up with his girlfriend over his claims that a wild wolf bit him. A tall tale considering wolves are extinct in the UK.

When he takes shelter from a storm in the house of wealthy landowner, Brian, he finds himself mysteriously drawn to the older man.

Find out what happens when Will is Bitten by the Alpha.

Bitten by the Alpha - Book 1

Claimed by the Alpha - Book 2

Trained by the Alpha - Book 3

Initiated by the Pack - Book 4

Submissive Lesbian Personal Assistant

This series is about Amber, a young woman who is seduced by her new employer, Susanna, a dominant and wealthy lesbian.

Her Lesbian Boss: The Complete Box Set

Books 1-6

Punished by Her Lesbian Boss

Seduced by Her Lesbian Boss

Trained by Her Lesbian Boss

Raced by Her Lesbian Boss

Shared by Her Lesbian Boss

Driven by Her Lesbian Boss

The Tribulations of Dawn

Dawn and the Galvanic Capacitor

Dawn and The Pilferer's Punishment

Dawn and the London Society

Dawn is a bounty hunter, bodyguard and private detective in a steampunk world full of adventure, excitement and lusty antics.

ABOUT THE AUTHOR

K.F. Jones writes in a wide variety of genres from paranormal romance, to steampunk, to reverse harem.

If you'd like to find out when new books are released, join the mailing list at the website.

http://kfjones.net/

twitter.com/kfjonesauthor
facebook.com/KFJonesbooks
pinterest.com/kfjonesauthor
goodreads.com/kfjones
amazon.com/author/kfjonesbooks